DINO
duckling

Alison Murray

ORCHARD

Even as an egg,

Dino Duckling was different.

TAP TAP

CRACK

DINO *duckling*

Alison Murray

For different ducks everywhere
A.M.

ORCHARD BOOKS

First published in Great Britain in 2017 by The Watts Publishing Group
This paperback edition first published in Great Britain in 2018

1 3 5 7 9 10 8 6 4 2

Text and illustrations © Alison Murray 2017

The moral rights of the author have been asserted.

A CIP catalogue record for this book is available from the British Library.

ISBN 978 1 40834 019 6

Printed and bound in China

MIX
Paper from
responsible sources
FSC® C104740
FSC
www.fsc.org

Orchard Books
An imprint of Hachette Children's Group
Part of The Watts Publishing Group Limited
Carmelite House
50 Victoria Embankment
London EC4Y 0DZ

An Hachette UK Company
www.hachette.co.uk
www.hachettechildrens.co.uk

BOOM

BOOM

CRUNCH

Dino Duckling started out big,

and then he **grew,**

and **grew,**

and . . .

GREW.

Sometimes Dino Duckling
couldn't help feeling different,
but Mama Duck always said,

"Big and wide,
sleek or slim,
we're a family
and we all fit in."

Different didn't make
any difference to her.

As spring turned to summer, Mama Duck taught her babies everything they needed to know.

How to **swim**,

how to **fish**,

how to **share**,

how to navigate
by the **stars**,

and how to
look out
for one another.

Most importantly, she taught them how to **celebrate their differences.**

Sadly not everyone
thought Dino Duckling belonged.
Sometimes **different** was . . .

difficult.

But Mama Duck just
gathered her babies
close and told them,

"Scales or feathers,
big or small,
we're a family
and there's room
for us all."

Summer turned to autumn, and soon it was time to fly south to the sunshine.

Dino Duckling **ran,**

and **jumped,**

and **flapped** . . .

But it was no good. Try as he might,
he simply **couldn't fly.**

Difference does matter,
thought Dino Duckling sadly.

As the leaves blew all around him, Dino Duckling lay down in the reeds and wept.

He imagined his
family far away.

But when he opened his eyes,
Dino Duckling got a
BIG surprise!
He saw . . .

1,2,3,4

faces he recognised!

They were all there.
The **WHOLE** family.

"We would
NEVER leave
without you,"
said Mama Duck.

"Fly or not,
it's all OK.
We're a family,
so we'll find a way."

And they did!